TO ALL THOSE LITTLE SPACE EXPLORERS OUT THERE.

MAYBE ONE OF YOU WILL MAKE THE TRIP TO MARS

—M. K.

FOR PAULA, TREVOR, AND EVAN,

WHO KEEP ME GROUNDED AND ALWAYS LOOKING UP

—C. F. P.

SIMON & SCHUSTER BOOKS FOR YOUNG READERS
An imprint of Simon & Schuster Children's Publishing Division
1230 Avenue of the Americas, New York, New York 10020
Text copyright © 2013 by Mark Kelly
Illustrations copyright © 2013 by C. F. Payne
All rights reserved, including the right of reproduction in whole or in part in any form.
SIMON & SCHUSTER BOOKS FOR YOUNG READERS is a trademark of Simon & Schuster, Inc.
For information about special discounts for bulk purchases, please contact Simon & Schuster Special Sales at 1-866-506-1949 or business@simonandschuster.com.
The Simon & Schuster Speakers Bureau can bring authors to your live event. For more information or to book an event, contact the Simon & Schuster Speakers Bureau at 1-866-248-3049 or visit our website at www.simonspeakers.com.
Book design by Lucy Ruth Cummins
The text for this book is set in Gotham.
The illustrations for this book are rendered in mixed media.
Manufactured in China
0713 SCP
2 4 6 8 10 9 7 5 3 1
CIP data for this book is available from the Library of Congress.
ISBN 978-1-4424-8426-9
ISBN 978-1-4424-8428-3 (eBook)

MOUSETRONAUT
GOES TO MARS

BY ASTRONAUT MARK KELLY

ILLUSTRATED BY

C. F. PAYNE

A PAULA WISEMAN BOOK
SIMON & SCHUSTER BOOKS FOR YOUNG READERS
New York London Toronto Sydney New Delhi

The *Galaxy Rocket* was just one week away from launching. It would be the first human mission to Mars. Even though Mars was Earth's neighbor, the astronauts would need to travel more than 35 million miles to get there.

And Meteor the Mousetronaut couldn't wait to go!

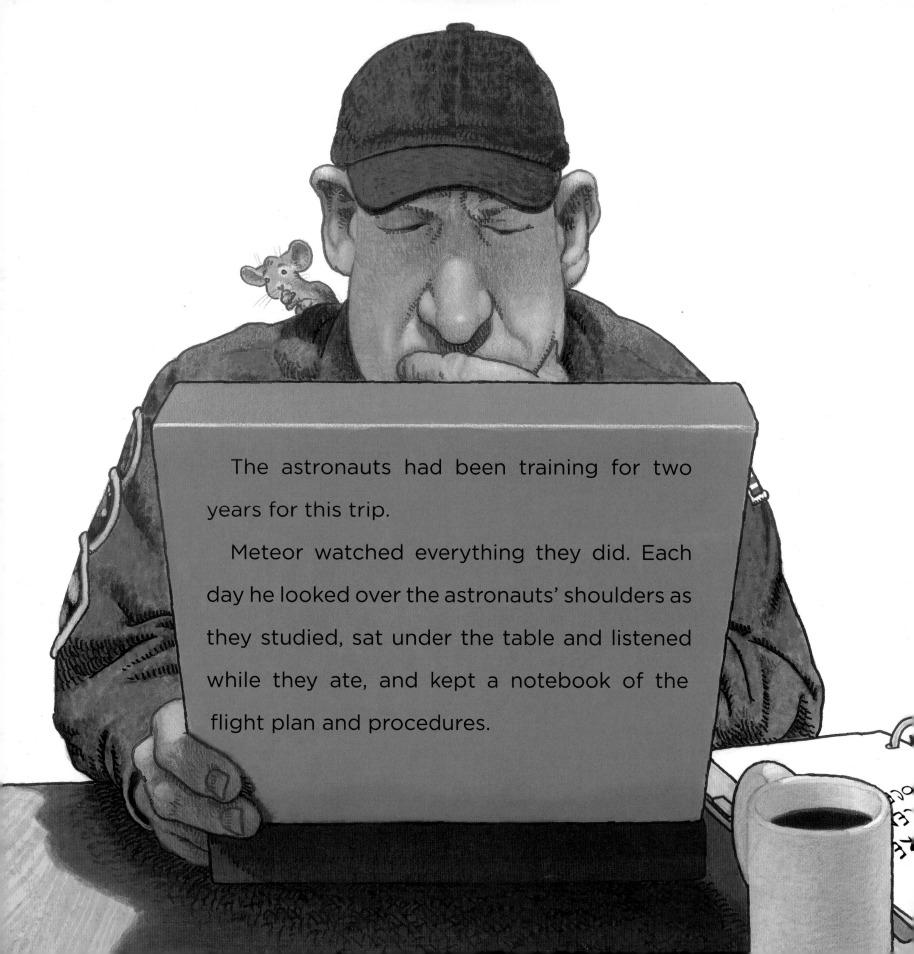

The astronauts had been training for two years for this trip.

Meteor watched everything they did. Each day he looked over the astronauts' shoulders as they studied, sat under the table and listened while they ate, and kept a notebook of the flight plan and procedures.

Meteor was certain that he'd be going to Mars too. He might not be the biggest astronaut, but he had the power of small.

He worked hard to stay in shape.

He ran with Claudia.

He did chin-ups with Claire.

He lifted weights with Charlotte.

The Mousetronaut was ready!

But when the names of the crew were called out, Meteor's name wasn't one of them. The Mousetronaut was not on the list.

NASA must have forgotten about their newest astronaut. There wasn't a chance Meteor was going to miss this exciting trip. He was small. He could hide. He would STOW AWAY!

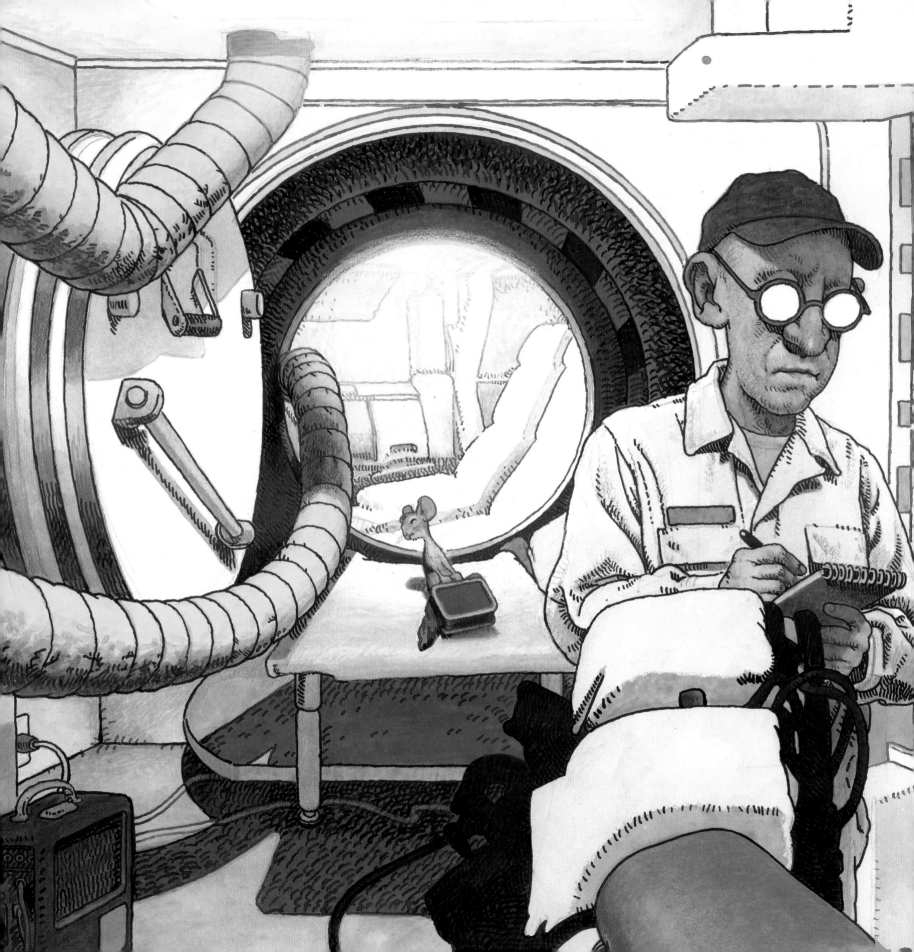

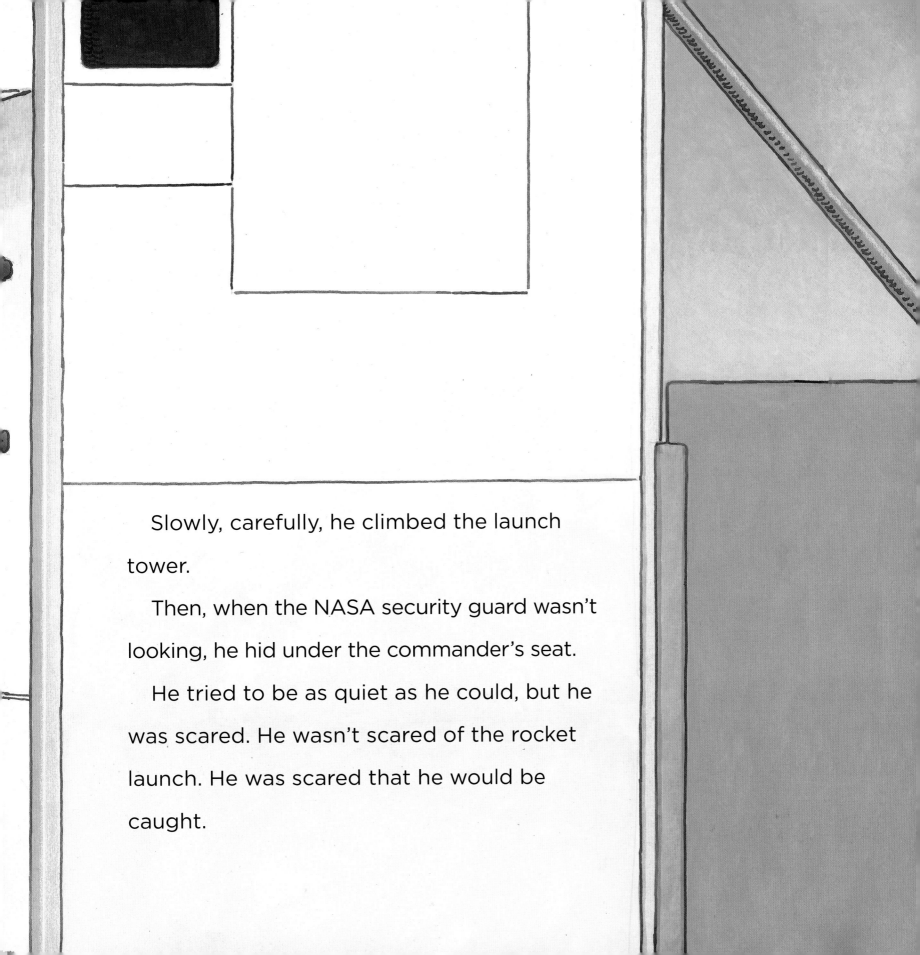

Slowly, carefully, he climbed the launch tower.

Then, when the NASA security guard wasn't looking, he hid under the commander's seat.

He tried to be as quiet as he could, but he was scared. He wasn't scared of the rocket launch. He was scared that he would be caught.

TEN–NINE–EIGHT–SEVEN–SIX–FIVE– FOUR–THREE–TWO–ONE...

LIFTOFF!

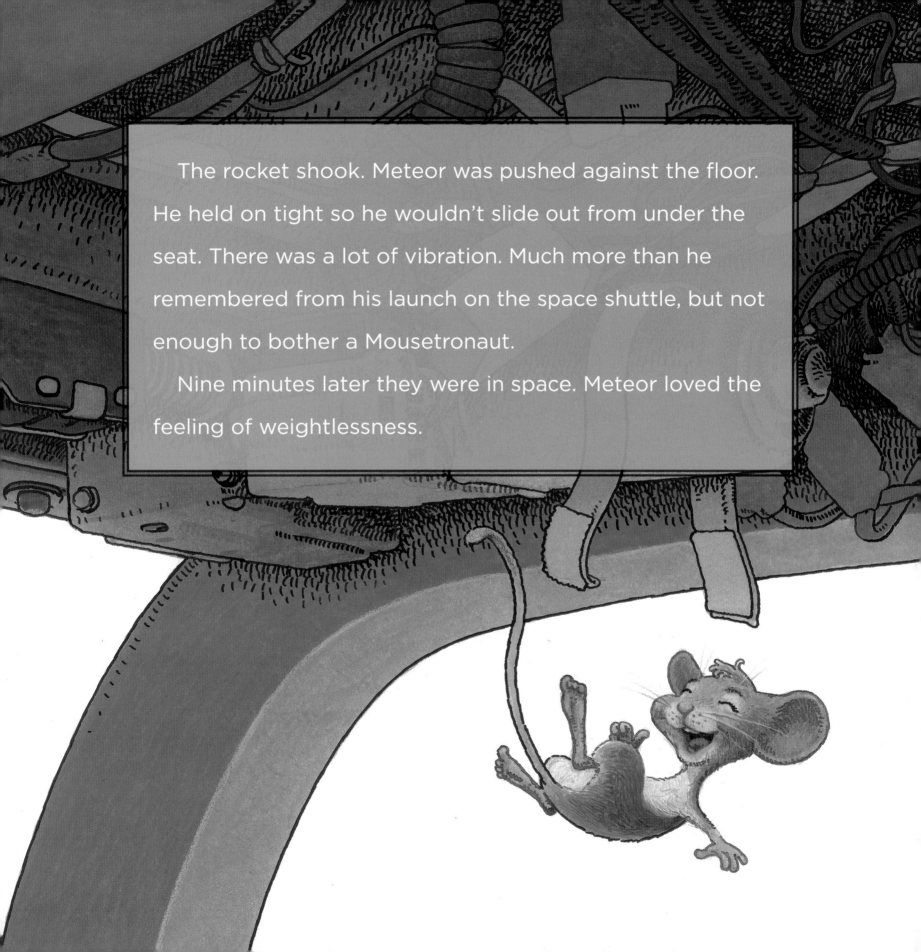

The rocket shook. Meteor was pushed against the floor. He held on tight so he wouldn't slide out from under the seat. There was a lot of vibration. Much more than he remembered from his launch on the space shuttle, but not enough to bother a Mousetronaut.

Nine minutes later they were in space. Meteor loved the feeling of weightlessness.

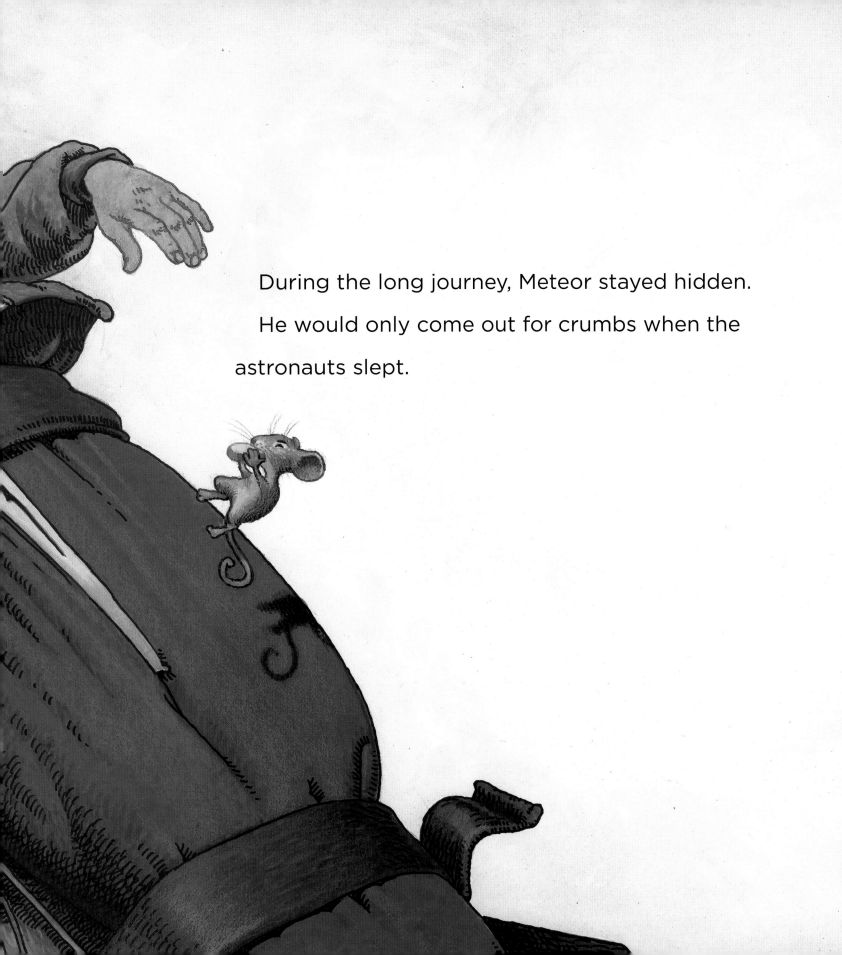

During the long journey, Meteor stayed hidden. He would only come out for crumbs when the astronauts slept.

And as Earth
got smaller
behind them,
the red dot
that was Mars
grew bigger.

After six months they finally arrived.

Meteor had stayed hidden the entire time.

When no one was looking, Meteor peeked
through the window and saw different shades
of red and orange.

Mars was nothing like Earth, but it was still
beautiful in its own way.

He also heard the astronauts making plans.

Two of them would go down to the surface
and explore Mars on foot and with a rover.

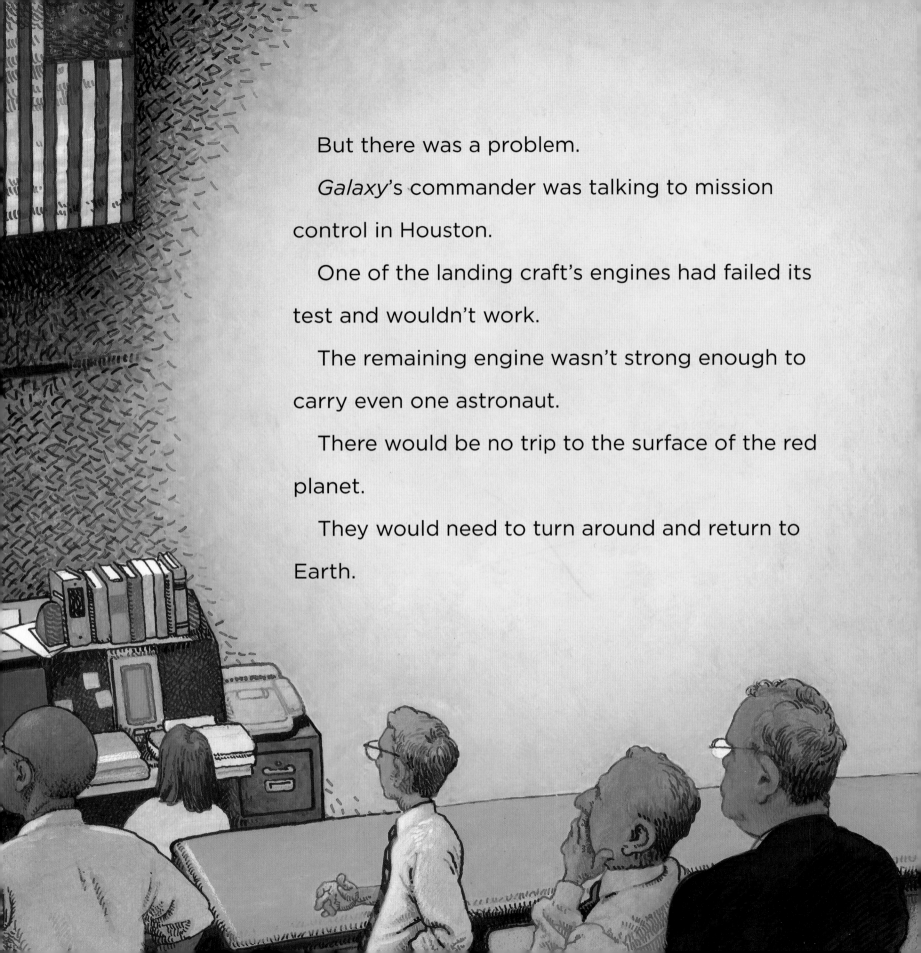

But there was a problem.

Galaxy's commander was talking to mission control in Houston.

One of the landing craft's engines had failed its test and wouldn't work.

The remaining engine wasn't strong enough to carry even one astronaut.

There would be no trip to the surface of the red planet.

They would need to turn around and return to Earth.

But the Moustronaut had an idea.
He shot out of his hiding place to
the surprise of the crew.
"Meteor! Where were you hiding?"
the commander asked.

They were happy to see him, but
still sad about their failed mission.
Then Meteor floated over to the
hatch leading to the landing craft.
"Hmm. It is possible," said
the commander. "One rocket
engine could work for
someone small enough."

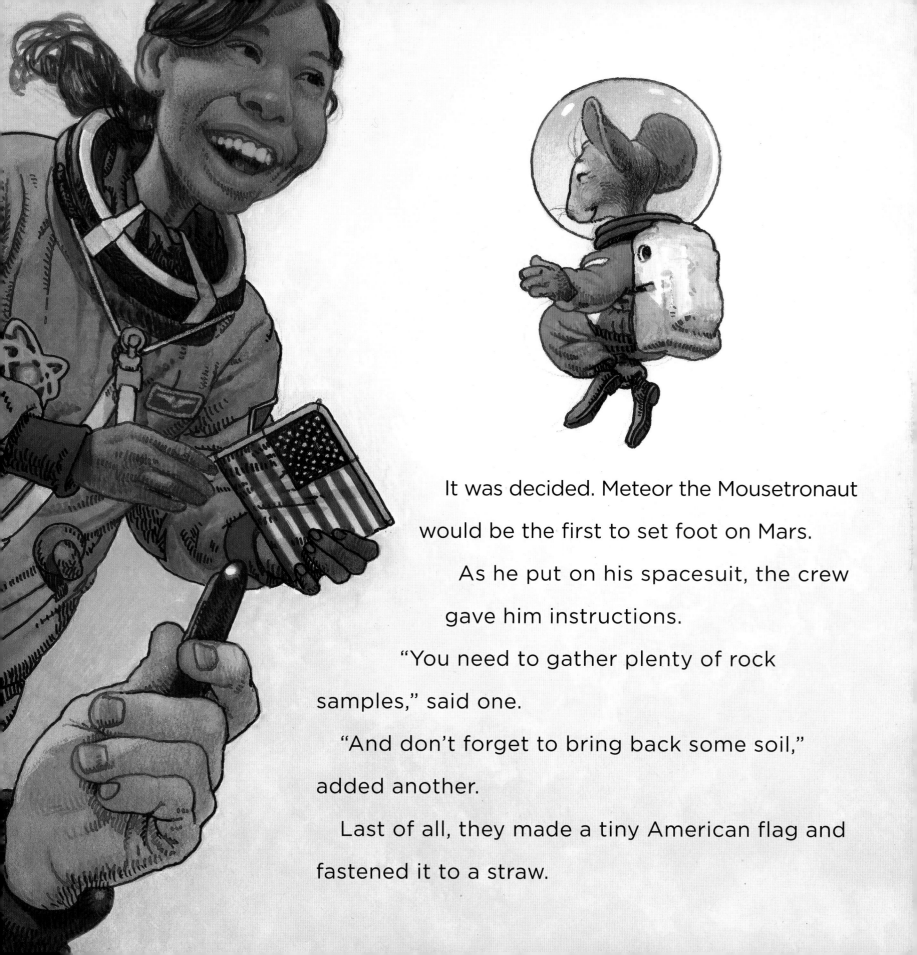

It was decided. Meteor the Mousetronaut would be the first to set foot on Mars.

As he put on his spacesuit, the crew gave him instructions.

"You need to gather plenty of rock samples," said one.

"And don't forget to bring back some soil," added another.

Last of all, they made a tiny American flag and fastened it to a straw.

Meteor tied himself into the seat of the landing craft with some string.

It launched from the *Galaxy* spacecraft and made its way to the surface of Mars.

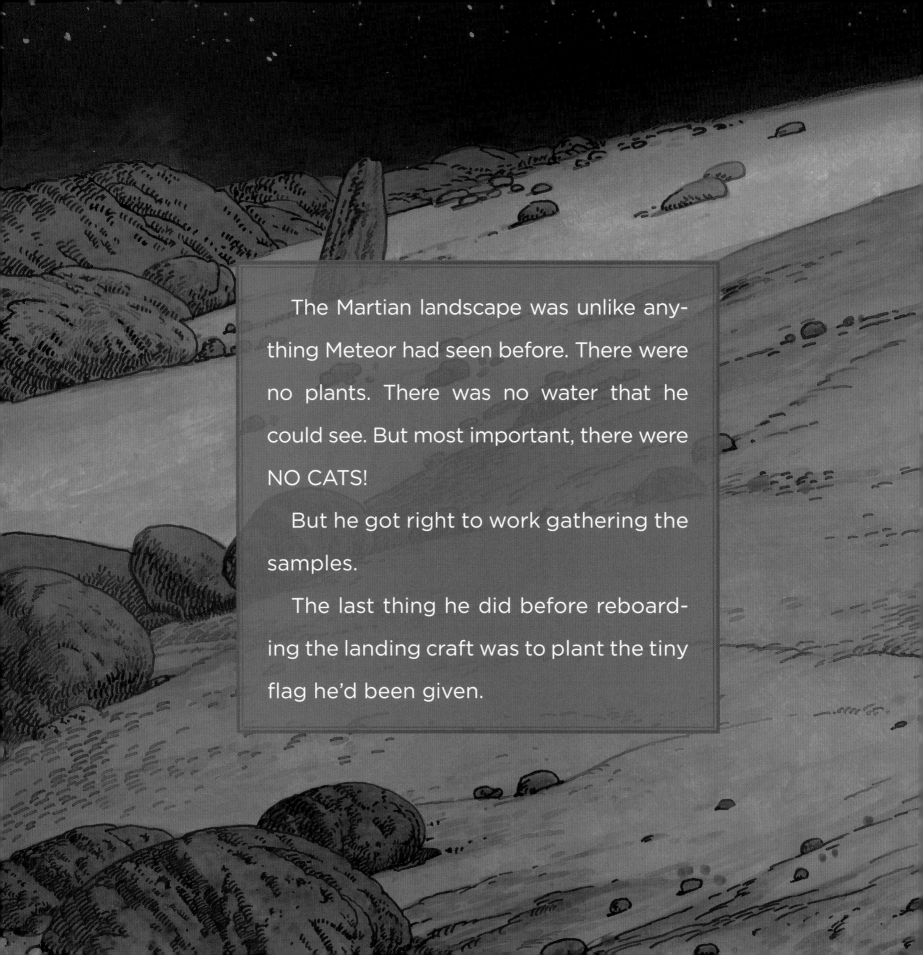

The Martian landscape was unlike anything Meteor had seen before. There were no plants. There was no water that he could see. But most important, there were NO CATS!

But he got right to work gathering the samples.

The last thing he did before reboarding the landing craft was to plant the tiny flag he'd been given.

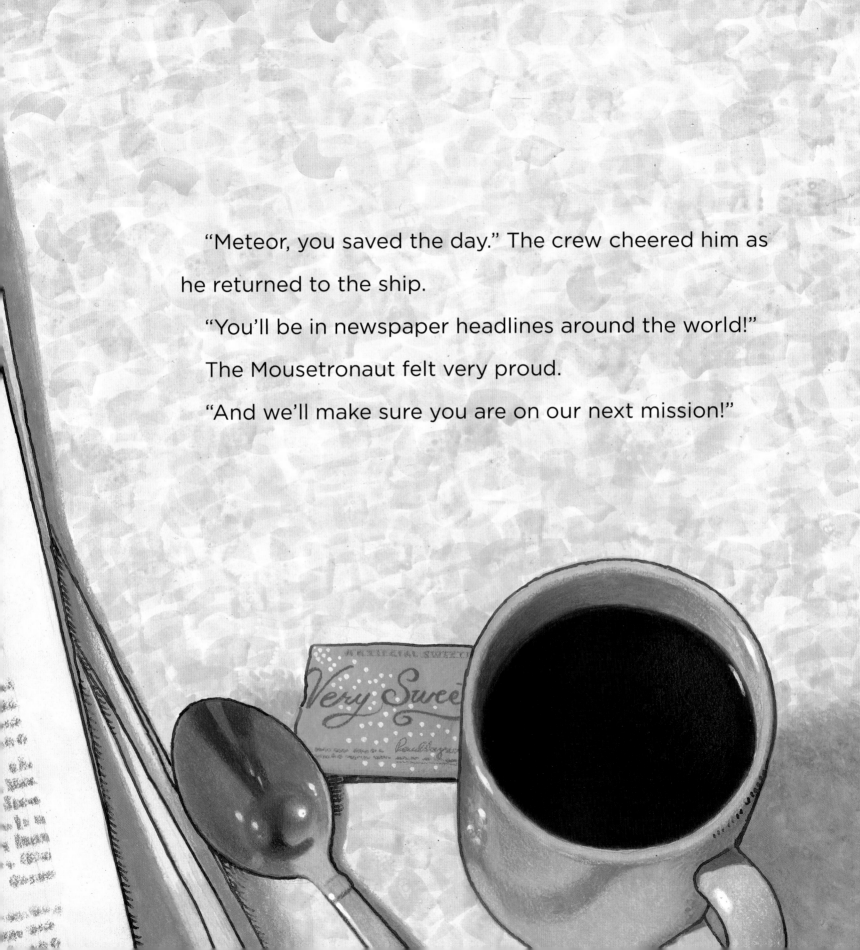

"Meteor, you saved the day." The crew cheered him as he returned to the ship.

"You'll be in newspaper headlines around the world!"

The Mousetronaut felt very proud.

"And we'll make sure you are on our next mission!"

Six months later *Galaxy Rocket* returned to Earth.

The astronauts were all welcomed as heroes.

But the smallest among them was the biggest hero of all.

AFTERWORD

Mars is one of the brightest objects in the night sky. It has long been an object of fascination and mystery. It shines with a reddish glow and is known as the Red Planet. The red color made ancient people think of blood and war. In fact, the Romans named Mars after their god of war. The color comes from the iron oxide (rust) that covers much of the planet's surface. The wind spreads the oxide dust and carries it into the atmosphere, where it reflects the red part of the light spectrum and causes the planet to appear red.

Mars can be seen by the naked eye, and it would have been visible to prehistoric man. Its presence was noted by ancient Egyptians, and it appears on the world's oldest star map, which dates back to 1500 BC By 400 BC Babylonian astronomers were able to study the planet's position and movements. They could even predict where it would be in the future.

The invention of the telescope in the seventeenth century finally allowed people a close-up view of the Red Planet. They could now see details of its surface. By the nineteenth century, improved telescopes revealed even more details, and in 1840 the first map of Mars was published. By the late 1800s scientists were able to see lines crisscrossing the planet. Some mistakenly identified them as man-made canals and thought they must have been dug to transport water across the planet. The idea of intelligent life on Mars took root and over time grew in the public's imagination. Some people imagined peaceful inhabitants on the planet. Others worried they might be warlike.

In 1938 a radio play of *The War of the Worlds*, a novel by H. G. Wells, envisioned Martians as warlike creatures. The public's fascination turned to panic when some people thought that the radio play was real and that Martians had actually reached Earth and landed in New Jersey!

Then in the 1950s, with the advent of the space program and travel to the Moon, the prospect of actually going *to* Mars was becoming a real possibility. Although observations with sophisticated telescopes told us a lot about the planet, the information to be gained from actually going there would be even more amazing. Most important, we could learn whether life existed (or ever did exist) on Mars.

However, travel to Mars is difficult, even for unmanned spacecraft. It is even more complex and difficult than going to the Moon. Besides the distance, it is complicated to rendezvous (meet up) with a planet that is also moving in space. You can't just fly to where the planet is; you have to fly to where it *will* be. It is essential to choose a route that takes the least time and uses the least amount of fuel. If the spacecraft had unlimited fuel and enough speed, it could chase the planet around the sun until it caught up. Since that is not possible, it is also essential to take off during the launch window, the time when Mars is at a point in its orbit that is closest to Earth (called opposition, or orbital alignment). The launch window for Mars occurs every twenty-six months, when Mars is about thirty-five million miles from Earth. Travel time varies between 150 and 300 days, depending on the speed of the spacecraft and the alignment of Earth and Mars.

The first successful flight to Mars was made by NASA's *Mariner 4* on a flyby mission. It flew by Mars in July 1965, 228 days after launching. It took twenty-one photographs (which disproved the theory of man-made canals on Mars). It was followed by *Mariner 6*, which reached the Red Planet in July 1969 after only 156 days in flight. In 1971 *Mariner 9* became the first spacecraft to successfully go into orbit around Mars.

Meanwhile the Soviets were also trying to send spacecraft to Mars. From the 1960s to 2011 they had eighteen failures and few successes. In November 1971 the Soviets managed to be the first to land a vehicle on Mars. Unfortunately, *Mars 2* crashed and *Mars 3* failed moments after its landing. After fifty years the Russians have yet to land successfully on Mars. To date, the United States is the only nation to have landed successfully on Mars.

In 1975 *Viking* orbiters and landers were sent to Mars and sent back over fifty thousand photographs. Orbiters are spacecraft that follow the planet's orbit and circle it, taking pictures and collecting information from above the surface of the planet. Landers actually set down on the surface of the planet. Sometimes they carry rovers, which can rove, or travel, on the surface of the planet.

Another milestone was the *Mars Pathfinder* lander, which carried the *Sojourner* rover (landed July 4, 1997). Air bags, similar to those in cars and what is used in Meteor's fictional landing, were used to soften the landing. The little rover traveled only about three hundred feet, but it provided a great deal of information and sent back 550 images.

Other successes followed, and as of 2012 there are two rovers on Mars actively sending signals and information back to Earth: *Opportunity* (landed in 2004) and *Curiosity* (2012). Plus there are three orbiters (*Mars Odyssey*, *Mars Express Orbiter*, and *Mars Reconnaissance Orbiter*) circling Mars and sending back information.

The rovers not only send back pictures, they also collect and analyze data. They use robotic arms to collect samples of rocks and soil, and use spectrometers and special rock crushers and other unique instruments to analyze the chemical components of the rocks, soil, and atmosphere. And in February 2013, *Curiosity* drilled the very first hole in Martian rock.

Each voyage has increased our knowledge about Mars. New information allows scientists to reevaluate theories and incorporate new facts. Detailed photographs have enabled them to map the surface of the planet with great accuracy. There is much they have learned.

Of all the planets in the solar system, Mars is the one most like Earth and the only one that might support life. Farther from the sun than Earth, Mars orbits (goes around) the sun in 687 days. That makes a Martian year almost twice as long as an Earth year. But a Martian day (called a sol) is almost the same. An Earth day is 23 hours, 56 minutes long. A Martian sol is 24 hours, 37.5 minutes long. While Earth has one Moon, Mars has two. Named after sons of the Greek god of war, these potato-shaped Moons (Phobos and Deimos) are both less than seventeen miles in diameter.

Mars is cold and its surface is rocky, dry, and dusty. It has the highest mountain in the solar system (about twice as tall as Mount Everest) and the biggest canyon (on Earth it would stretch from New York to California).

Mars is about half the size of Earth and its gravity is about 40 percent of Earth's gravity. A person weighing

100 pounds on Earth would weigh only 40 pounds on Mars. If people lived on Mars, they would be able to jump higher and lift bigger objects. However, because of the air's chemical composition (ten times as much carbon dioxide and virtually no oxygen) and its thinness, they wouldn't be able to breathe the air and would have to wear protective clothing (spacesuits) to survive. Without a spacesuit, the low air pressure would cause a person's blood to boil! The climate would also be a challenge. A warm summer's day might be in the seventies, but the winter nights can reach minus 225 degrees—brrrr!

Of all the many exciting things the orbiters and rovers have found out, none is more important than the confirmation that liquid water once existed on Mars (determined by *Curiosity* in 2012). This is important because water is essential to life on Earth. On Earth life exists almost everywhere that water does. Could this mean that life exists on Mars (maybe under the surface of the planet) or that life once existed in the past? This probably doesn't mean life as we know it; nevertheless, even if it is simple cells or bacteria, this is a thrilling idea. If there is life on Mars, it increases the chance that there is other life in the universe—maybe even intelligent life!

As amazing as all the discoveries have been, there is so much more to learn. By studying Mars, who knows what can be discovered about its geology, evolution, and climate change, and what that might tell us about the history and future of Earth and of life itself.

While rovers and robotic technology can tell us a lot, there are limits to what they can do. It takes an average of four to fourteen minutes for signals to reach Mars from Earth. Depending on where each planet is in its own orbit, the distance between them changes, and thus, the travel time for the signal to reach its destination. Don't forget to add on another four to fourteen minutes for the signal's return trip to Earth. This is a significant delay and makes it impractical to control everything from Earth. Without instant feedback, robotic explorers like the rovers can have trouble making quick decisions—for example, whether to go over or around an obstacle. A wrong choice could tip the vehicle over. Human beings, on the other hand, can process information and act immediately. There is no fourteen-minute delay, and they can act in unexpected circumstances without having their software updated or reprogrammed. This is a valuable asset on an expedition of exploration.

Although human beings (and mice) have yet to go to Mars, plans are already being made to change that. But the challenges are many. For starters, the voyage is long (about two years). Imagine being in a cramped, close space, far away from family and friends, for that long. It will be important for crew members to be both cooperative and self-reliant. They will need to have a good sense of humor. Thoughtfulness and being considerate of one another will also be important, since there is no place for a time-out on a spacecraft.

Also, the spacecraft will be carrying supplies as well as people and will need a great deal of fuel for the long flight there and back. Scientists and engineers will need to design a spacecraft that can carry enough fuel and that will be able to land and take off to get back to Earth. The crew won't be able to take along enough food— even freeze-dried food would weigh too much. So we are not sure how to feed a crew in space for such a long journey. One option is to bring all the food for such an extended trip. But food is heavy, so NASA is also look-